For Antonia Louise
J.S.

For Muggs, a princess among turtles!
T.W.

First edition published 2001
in Great Britain by Penguin Books Ltd
Middlesex, England

First edition for the United States and Canada published 2001 by
Barron's Educational Series, Inc.

All inquiries should be addressed to:
Barron's Educational Series, Inc.
250 Wireless Boulevard
Hauppauge, New York 11788
http://www.barronseduc.com

Library of Congress Catalog Card No. 00-109383
International Standard Book No. 0-7641-5347-1

Printed in U A E
1 3 5 7 9 10 8 6 4 2

That's Not Fair, Hare!

Julie Sykes

Illustrated by Tim Warnes

One day, Muggs the turtle plodded down to the farmer's cabbage field as usual for her lunch. When she got there she found a greedy young hare wolfing down all the cabbages.

"Slow down!" cried Muggs. "If you eat that quickly there won't be any left for me."

"Too bad," said Hare. "I was here first."

"That's not very nice," said Muggs. "There are enough cabbages for both of us if we share them."

But Hare was very greedy and he didn't want to share.

"I've got a much better idea," he said craftily.

"Let's have a race," said Hare. "Meet me tomorrow morning at my home under the oak tree. The first one to reach the farmer's field is the winner and gets to eat all the cabbages."

"It would be nicer to share," answered Muggs. "Besides, your legs are longer than mine so you can run much faster."

But Hare wouldn't change his mind.

"If you don't race, then I'll get all the cabbages," he said.

So Muggs agreed to the race.

By the next morning, everyone had heard about the race and several animals were gathered under the oak tree to cheer Muggs on. Slowly, Muggs made her way to the start line. Hare was waiting there, chewing on a blade of grass.

"Hurry up, Speedy, or we'll be racing by moonlight," he taunted.

Rabbit started them off. "READY, SET, GO!" she cried.
At once, Hare zoomed off, shouting rudely, "See you tomorrow, Turtle, or will it be next week?"

Muggs started to crawl after him, but Rabbit stopped her.
"You'll never get anywhere if you go that slowly," she said. "To go quickly you must hop, like this."

Rabbit began to hop along the path, calling words of encouragement to Muggs.

"Back legs higher," she shouted. "Hop, hop, hop!"

Rabbit was so busy watching Muggs, she wasn't looking where she was going.

CRASH!

She hopped right off the path and tumbled into a ditch.

"Help," she cried. "I'm stuck!"

Muggs sighed. She didn't really have time to stop, but Rabbit was only trying to help and Muggs couldn't leave her in the ditch. Carefully, she plodded over to the edge and reached for Rabbit's paw.

Muggs p-u-l-l-e-d and *tugged* and *tugged* and p-u-l-l-e-d and at last Rabbit was able to climb safely back onto the path.

Squirrel was waiting for them.

"You'll never win the race if you keep stopping," he chattered. "Running is easy. Follow me and I'll show you what to do."

Squirrel scampered along, calling behind him, "skip, skip, skip!"

But he wasn't watching where he was going.

BANG!

He tripped over a tree root and landed in a thorn bush.

"Ouch!" he cried. "Help, I'm stuck!"

"Bother!" said Muggs.

The thorns didn't worry her, not with her hard shell, but helping Squirrel was going to hold her up even more!

I'm never going to win this race now, she thought, but still Muggs crawled into the bush and held back the branches so that Squirrel could scramble out.

Slowly, Muggs plodded back to the path.

"Hop," called Rabbit encouragingly. "Hop, hop, hop!"
"No, skip!" shouted Squirrel."Skip, skip, skip!"
Muggs didn't think she would win the race, but she wasn't going to give up yet.

While Rabbit and Squirrel argued, she trudged through the woods as fast as her legs could carry her. When she reached the edge of the trees Muggs could hardly believe her eyes. There she saw . . .

. . . Hare, asleep by the stream.

Rabbit and Squirrel stopped arguing.
"Hooray!" they cheered. "You can do it. You can still win the race!"

Muggs walked steadily on. She crept past sleeping Hare and over the bridge. It was only a little bit farther to the farmer's cabbage field. Muggs could smell those cabbages! She was almost there when . . .

. . . Rabbit and Squirrel cheered so loudly they woke Hare up.

Quickly he scrambled to his paws and overtook Muggs, just before she reached the cabbage field.

"I won," said Hare smugly.
"The cabbages are all mine."

"But that's not fair!" Rabbit was very angry. "You only won because we woke you up."

"True," said Hare. "But I'm still the winner."

Suddenly Muggs had a clever idea.

"Let's race again," she suggested. "Only this time the winner gets the cabbages *and* that field of carrots next door."

Greedily, Hare licked his lips.

"All right. I'm bound to win. So where shall we race to this time?"

"Home," said Muggs.

"Those cabbages and carrots are already mine!" said Hare.

"We'll see," Muggs replied.

"READY . . . SET . . .

. . . GO!"

"I won!" said Muggs, pulling her legs into her shell.
And she had, because she was already home.